Uncle Tom's Cabin, Young Folks' Edition

Harriet Beecher Stowe

Abolitionist author, Harriet Beecher Stowe rose to fame in 1851 with the publication of her best-selling book, Uncle Tom's Cabin, which highlighted the evils of slavery, angered the slaveholding South, and inspired pro-slavery copy-cat works in defense of the institution of slavery.

Stowe was born on June 14, 1811 in Litchfield, Connecticut, the seventh child of famed Congregational minister Lyman Beecher and Roxana Foote Beecher. Her famous siblings include elder sister Catherine (11 years her senior), and Henry Ward Beecher, the famous preacher and reformer. Stowe's mother died when she was five years old and while her father remarried, her sister Catherine became the most pronounced influence on young Harriet's life. At age eight, she began her education at the Litchfield

Female Academy. Later, in 1824, she attended Catherine Beecher's Hartford Female Seminary, which exposed young women to many of the same courses available in men's academies. Stowe's proclivity for writing was evident in the essays she produced for school. Stowe became a teacher, working from 1829 to 1832 at the Hartford Female Seminary.

In 1832, when Stowe's father Lyman accepted the position of president of the esteemed Lane Seminary in Cincinnati, Ohio, she went with him. There, she met some of the great minds and reformers of the day, including noted abolitionists. Smitten with the landscape of the West, she published her first book, Primary Geography, in 1833, which celebrated the diverse cultures and vistas she encountered. In 1836, she met and married Calvin Stowe, a professor at the Lane Seminary. He encouraged her writing, they had seven children, and weathered financial and other problems during their decades-long union. Stowe would write countless articles, some were published in the renowned women's magazine of the times, Godey's Lady's Book. She also wrote 30 books, covering a wide range of topics from homemaking to religion in nonfiction, as well as several novels.

The turning point in Stowe's personal and literary life came in 1849, when her son died in a cholera epidemic that claimed nearly 3000 lives in her region. She later said that the loss of her child inspired great empathy for enslaved mothers who had their children sold away from them. The passage of the Fugitive Slave Act of 1850, which legally compelled Northerners to return runaway slaves, infuriated Stowe and many in the North. This was when Stowe penned what would become her most famous work, the novel, Uncle Tom's Cabin. Originally serialized in the National Era, Stowe saw her tale as a call to arms for Northerners to defy the Fugitive Slave Act. The vivid characters and great empathy inspired by the book was further aided by Stowe's strong Christianity.

Uncle Tom's Cabin was released as a book in March 1852, selling 300,000 copies in the US in the first year. It was later performed on stage and translated into dozens of languages. When some claimed her portrait of slavery was inaccurate, Stowe published Key to Uncle Tom's Cabin, a book of primary source historical documents that backed up her account, including the narratives of notable former slaves Frederick Douglass and Josiah Henderson. Southern pro-slavery advocates countered with books of their own, such as Mary Henderson Eastman's Aunt Phillis's Cabin; Or, Southern Life as It Is. This work and others like it attempted to portray slavery as a benevolent institution, but never received the acclaim or widespread readership of Stowe's.

Stowe used her fame to petition to end slavery. She toured nationally and internationally, speaking about her book and donating some of what she earned to help the antislavery cause. She also wrote extensively on behalf of abolition, most notably her "Appeal to Women of the Free States of America, on the Present Crisis on Our Country," which she hoped would help raise public outcry to defeat the 1854 Kansas-Nebraska Act.

During the Civil War, Stowe became one of the most visible professional writers. For years, popular folklore claimed that President Abraham Lincoln, upon meeting Stowe in 1862, said, "So you're the woman who wrote the book that started this great war." That quote, published in a 1911 biography of Stowe by her son Charles, has been called into question, as Stowe herself and two others present at the meeting make no reference to it in their accounts (and Charles was only a boy at the time of the meeting).

In 1873, Stowe and her family moved to Hartford, Connecticut, where she remained until her death in 1896, summering in Florida. She helped breathe new life into the Wadsworth Atheneum Museum of Art, and was involved with efforts to launch the Hartford Art School, later part of the University of Hartford.

CHAPTER I

UNCLE TOM AND LITTLE HARRY ARE SOLD

V

ERY many years ago, instead of having servants to wait upon them and work for them, people used to have slaves. These slaves were paid no wages. Their masters gave them only food and clothes in return for their work.

When any one wanted servants he went to market to buy them, just as nowadays we buy horses and cows, or even tables and chairs.

If the poor slaves were bought by kind people they would be quite happy. Then they would work willingly for their masters and mistresses, and even love them. But very often cruel people bought slaves. These cruel people used to beat them and be unkind to them in many other ways.

It was very wicked to buy and sell human beings as if they were cattle. Yet Christian people did it, and many who were good and kind otherwise thought there was no wrong in being cruel to their poor slaves. 'They are only black people,' they said to themselves. 'Black people do not feel things as we do.' That was not kind, as black people suffer pain just in the same way as white people do.

One of the saddest things for the poor slaves was that they could never long be a happy family all together—father, mother, and little brothers and sisters—because at any time the master might sell the father or the mother or one of the children to some one else. When this happened those who were left behind were very sad indeed—more sad than if their dear one had died.

Uncle Tom was a slave. He was a very faithful and honest servant, and his master, Mr. Shelby, was kind to him. Uncle Tom's wife was called Aunt Chloe. She was Mr. Shelby's head cook, and a very good one too, she was. Nobody in all

8

the country round could make such delicious pies and cakes as Aunt Chloe.

Uncle Tom and Aunt Chloe lived together in a pretty little cottage built of wood, quite close to Mr. Shelby's big house.

The little cottage was covered with climbing roses, and the garden was full of beautiful bright flowers and lovely fruit trees.

Uncle Tom and Aunt Chloe lived happily for many years in their little cottage, or cabin, as it was called. All day Uncle Tom used to work in the fields, while Aunt Chloe was busy in the kitchen at Mr. Shelby's house. When evening came they both went home to their cottage and their children, and were merry together.

Mr. Shelby was a good man, and kind to his slaves, but he was not very careful of his money. When he had spent all he had, he did not know what to do to get more. At last he borrowed money from a man called Haley, hoping to be able to pay it back again some day.

But that day never came. Haley grew impatient, and said, 'If you don't pay what you owe me, I will take your house and lands, and sell them to pay myself back all the money I have lent to you.'

So Mr. Shelby sold everything he could spare and gathered money together in every way he could think of, but still there was not enough.

Then Haley said, 'Give me that slave of yours called Tom—he is worth a lot of money.'

But Mr. Shelby knew that Haley was not a nice man. He knew he did not want

Tom for a servant, but only wanted to sell him again, to make more money. So Mr. Shelby said, 'No, I can't do that. I never mean to sell any of my slaves, least of all Tom. He has been with me since he was a little boy.'

'Oh very well,' said Haley, 'I shall sell your house and lands, as I said I should.'

Mr. Shelby could not bear to think of that, so he agreed to let Haley have Tom. He made him promise, however, not to sell Tom again except to a kind master.

'Very well,' said Haley, 'but Tom isn't enough. I must have another slave.'

Just at this moment a little boy came dancing into the room where Mr. Shelby and Haley were talking.

He was a pretty, merry little fellow, the son of a slave called Eliza, who was Mrs. Shelby's maid.

'There now,' said Haley, 'give me that little chap, as well as Tom, and we will say no more about the money you owe me.'

'I can't,' said Mr. Shelby. 'My wife is very fond of Eliza, and would never hear of having Harry sold.'

'Oh, very well,' said Haley once more, 'I must just sell your house.'

So again Mr. Shelby gave in, and Haley went away with the promise that next morning Uncle Tom and little Harry should be given to him, to be his slaves.

Eliza was going to run away.

She gathered a few of Harry's clothes into a bundle, put on her hat and jacket, and went to wake him.

Poor Harry was rather frightened at being waked in the middle of the night, and at seeing his mother bending over him, with her hat and jacket on.

'What is the matter, mother?' he said beginning to cry.

'Hush,' she said, 'Harry mustn't cry or speak aloud, or they will hear us. A wicked man was coming to take little Harry away from his mother, and carry him 'way off in the dark. But mother won't let him. She's going to put on her little boy's cap and coat, and run off with him, so the ugly man can't catch him.'

Harry stopped crying at once, and was good and quiet as a little mouse, while his mother dressed him. When he was ready, she lifted him in her arms, and crept softly out of the house.

It was a beautiful, clear, starlight night, but very cold, for it was winter-time. Eliza ran quickly to Uncle Tom's cottage, and tapped on the window.

Aunt Chloe was not asleep, so she jumped up at once, and opened the door. She was very much astonished to see Eliza standing there with Harry in her arms. Uncle Tom followed her to the door, and was very much astonished too.

'I'm running away, Uncle Tom and Aunt Chloe—carrying off my child,' said Eliza. 'Master sold him.'

'Sold him?' they both echoed, lifting up their hands in dismay.

'Yes, sold him,' said Eliza. 'I heard master tell missis that he had sold my Harry, and you, Uncle Tom. The man is coming to take you away to-morrow.'

At first Tom could hardly believe what he heard. Then he sank down, and buried his face in his hands.

'The good Lord have pity on us!' said Aunt Chloe. 'What has Tom done that master should sell him?'

'He hasn't done anything—it isn't for that. Master don't want to sell; but he owes this man money. If he doesn't pay him it will end in his having to sell the house and all the slaves. Master said he was sorry. But missis she talked like an angel. I'm a wicked girl to leave her so, but I can't help it. It must be right; but if it an't right, the good Lord will forgive me, for I can't help doing it.

'Tom,' said Aunt Chloe, 'why don't you go too? There's time.'

Tom slowly raised his head and looked sorrowfully at her.

'No, no,' he said. 'Let Eliza go. It is right that she should try to save her boy. Mas'r has always trusted me, and I can't leave him like that. It is better for me to go alone than for the whole place to be sold. Mas'r isn't to blame, Chloe. He will take

14

care of you and the poor—'

Tom could say no more. Big man though he was, he burst into tears, at the thought of leaving his wife and dear little children, never to see them any more.

'Aunt Chloe,' said Eliza, in a minute or two, 'I must go. I saw my husband to-day. He told me he meant to run away soon, because his master is so cruel to him. Try to send him a message from me. Tell him I have run away to save our boy. Tell him to come after me if he can. Good-bye, good-bye. God bless you!'

Then Eliza went out again into the dark night with her little boy in her arms, and Aunt Chloe shut the door softly behind her.

CHAPTER III

THE MORNING AFTER

Next morning, when it was discovered that Eliza had run away with her little boy, there was great excitement and confusion all over the house.

Mrs. Shelby was very glad. 'Thank God!' she said. 'I hope Eliza will get right away. I could not bear to think of Harry being sold to that cruel man.'

Mr. Shelby was angry. 'Haley knew I didn't want to sell the child,' he said. 'He will blame me for this.'

One person only was quite silent, and that was Aunt Chloe. She went on, making the breakfast as if she heard and saw nothing of the excitement round her.

All the little black boys belonging to the house thought it was fine fun. Very soon, about a dozen young imps were roosting, like so many crows, on the railings, waiting for Haley to come. They wanted to see how angry he would be, when he heard the news.

And he was dreadfully angry. The little nigger boys thought it was grand. They shouted and laughed and made faces at him to their hearts' content.

At last Haley became so angry, that Mr. Shelby offered to give him two men to help him to find Eliza.

But these two men, Sam and Andy, knew quite well that Mrs. Shelby did not want Eliza to be caught, so they put off as much time as they could.

They let loose their horses and Haley's too. Then they frightened and chased them, till they raced like mad things all over the great lawns which surrounded the house.

Whenever it seemed likely that a horse would be caught, Sam ran up, waving his hat and shouting wildly, 'Now for it! Cotch him! Cotch him!' This frightened the horses so much that they galloped off faster than before.

Haley rushed up and down, shouting and using dreadful, naughty words, and stamping with rage all the time.

At last, about twelve o'clock, Sam came riding up with Haley's horse. 'He's cotched,' he said, seemingly very proud of himself. 'I cotched him!'

Of course, now it was too late to start before dinner. Besides, the horses were so tired with all their running about, that they had to have a rest.

When at last they did start, Sam led them by a wrong road. So the sun was almost setting before they arrived at the village where Haley hoped to find Eliza.

CHAPTER IV

THE CHASE

When Eliza left Uncle Tom's cabin, she felt very sad and lonely. She knew she was leaving all the friends she had ever had behind her.

At first Harry was frightened. Soon he grew sleepy. 'Mother, I don't need to keep awake, do I?' he said.

'No, my darling, sleep, if you want to.'

'But, mother, if I do get asleep, you won't let the bad man take me?'

'No!'

'You're sure, an't you, mother?'

'Yes, sure.'

Harry dropped his little weary head upon her shoulder, and was soon fast asleep.

Eliza walked on and on, never resting, all through the night. When the sun rose, she was many miles away from her old home. Still she walked on, only stopping, in the middle of the day, to buy a little dinner for herself and Harry at a farm-house.

At last, when it was nearly dark, she arrived at a village, on the banks of the river Ohio. If she could only get across that river, Eliza felt she would be safe.

She went to a little inn on the bank, where a kind-looking woman was busy cooking supper.

'Is there a boat that takes people across the river now?' she asked.

'No, indeed,' replied the woman. 'The boats has stopped running. It isn't safe, there be too many blocks of ice floating about.'

Eliza looked so sad and disappointed when she heard this, that the good woman was sorry for her. Harry too was so tired, that he began to cry.

'Here, take him into this room,' said the woman, opening the door into a small bed-room.

Eliza laid her tired little boy upon the bed, and he soon fell fast asleep. But for her there was no rest. She stood at the window, watching the river with its great floating blocks of ice, wondering how she could cross it.

As she stood there she heard a shout. Looking up she saw Sam. She drew back just in time, for Haley and Andy were riding only a yard or two behind him.

It was a dreadful moment for Eliza. Her room opened by a side door to the river. She seized her child and sprang down the steps towards it.

Haley caught sight of her as she disappeared down the bank. Throwing himself from his horse, and calling loudly to Sam and Andy, he was after her in a moment.

In that terrible moment her feet scarcely seemed to touch the ground. The next, she was at the water's edge.

On they came behind her. With one wild cry and flying leap, she jumped right over the water by the shore, on to the raft of ice beyond. It was a desperate leap. Haley, Sam, and Andy cried out, and lifted up their hands in astonishment.

The great piece of ice pitched and creaked as her weight came upon it. But she stayed there not a moment. With wild cries she leaped to another and still another — stumbling — leaping — slipping — springing up again!

Her shoes were gone, her stockings cut from her feet by the sharp edges of the ice. Blood marked every step. But she knew nothing, felt nothing, till dimly, as in a dream, she saw the Ohio side, and a man helping her up the bank.

'Yer a brave gal, now, whoever ye are!' said the man.

'Oh, save me — do save me — do hide me,' she cried.

'Why, what's the matter?' asked the man.

'My child! this boy — mas'r sold him. There's his new mas'r,' she said, pointing to the other shore. 'Oh, save me.'

'Yer a right brave gal,' said the man. 'Go there,' pointing to a big white house close by. 'They are kind folks; they'll help you.'

'Oh, thank you, thank you,' said Eliza, as she walked quickly away. The man stood and looked after her wonderingly.

On the other side of the river Haley was standing perfectly amazed at the scene. When Eliza disappeared over the bank he turned and looked at Sam and Andy, with terrible anger in his eyes.

But Sam and Andy were glad, oh, so glad, that Eliza had escaped. They were so glad that they laughed till the tears rolled down their cheeks.

'I'll make ye laugh,' said Haley, laying about their heads with his riding whip.

They ducked their heads, ran shouting up the bank, and were on their horses before he could reach them.

'Good evening, mas'r,' said Sam. 'I berry much 'spect missis be anxious 'bout us. Mas'r Haley won't want us no longer.' Then off they went as fast as their horses could gallop.

It was late at night before they reached home again, but Mrs. Shelby was waiting for them. As soon as she heard the horses galloping up she ran out to the balcony.

'Is that you, Sam?' she called. 'Where are they?'

'Mas'r Haley's a-restin' at the tavern. He's drefful fatigued, missis.'

'And Eliza, Sam?'

'Come up here, Sam,' called Mr. Shelby, who had followed his wife, 'and tell your mistress what she wants to know.'

So Sam went up and told the wonderful story of how Eliza had crossed the river on the floating ice. Mr. and Mrs. Shelby found it hard to believe that such a thing was possible.

Mrs. Shelby was very, very glad that Eliza had escaped. She told Aunt Chloe to give Sam and Andy a specially good supper. Then they went to bed quite pleased with their day's work.

CHAPTER V

ELIZA FINDS A REFUGE

A lady and gentleman were sitting talking happily together in the drawing-room of the white house to which Eliza had gone. Suddenly their old black man-of-all-work put his head in at the door and said, 'Will missis come into the kitchen?'

The lady went. Presently she called to her husband, 'I do wish you would come here a moment.'

He rose and went into the kitchen.

There lay Eliza on two kitchen chairs. Her poor feet were all cut and bleeding, and she had fainted quite away. The master of the house drew his breath short, and stood silent.

His wife and the cook were trying to bring Eliza round. The old man had Harry on his knee, and was busy pulling off his shoes and stockings, to warm the little cold feet.

'Poor creature,' said the lady.

Suddenly Eliza opened her eyes. A dreadful look of pain came into her face. She sprang up saying, 'Oh, my Harry, have they got him?'

As soon as he heard her voice, Harry jumped from the old man's knee, and running to her side, put up his arms.

'Oh, he's here! he's here,' she said, kissing him. 'Oh, ma'am,' she went, on turning wildly to the lady of the house, 'do protect us, don't let them get him.'

'Nobody shall hurt you here, poor woman,' said the lady. 'You are safe; don't be afraid.'

'God bless you,' said Eliza, covering her face and sobbing, while Harry, seeing her crying, tried to get into her lap to comfort her.

'You needn't be afraid of anything; we are friends here, poor woman. Tell me where you come from and what you want,' said the lady.

'I came from the other side of the river,' said Eliza.

'When?' said the gentleman, very much astonished.

'To-night.'

'How did you come?'

'I crossed on the ice.'

'Crossed on the ice!' exclaimed every one.

'Yes,' said Eliza slowly, 'I did. God helped me, and I crossed on the ice. They were close behind me—right behind, and there was no other way.'

'Law, missis,' said the old servant, 'the ice is all in broken up blocks, a-swinging up and down in the water.'

'I know it is. I know it,' said Eliza wildly. 'But I did it. I would'nt have thought I could—I didn't think I could get over, but I didn't care. I could but die if I didn't. And God helped me.'

'Were you a slave?' said the gentleman.

'Yes, sir.'

'Was your master unkind to you?'

'No, sir.'

'Was your mistress unkind to you?'

'No, sir — no. My mistress was always good to me.'

'What could make you leave a good home, then, and run away, and go through such danger?'

'They wanted to take my boy away from me — to sell him — to sell him down south, ma'am. To go all alone — a baby that had never been away from his mother in his life. I couldn't bear it. I took him, and ran away in the night. They chased me, they were coming down close behind me, and I heard 'em. I jumped right on to the ice. How I got across I don't know. The first I knew, a man was helping me up the bank.'

It was such a sad story, that the tears came into the eyes of everyone who heard her tell it.

'Where do you mean to go to, poor woman?' asked the lady.

'To Canada, if I only knew where that was. Is it very far off, is Canada'? said Eliza, looking up in a simple, trusting way, to the kind lady's face.

'Poor woman,' said she again.

'Is it a great way off?' asked Eliza.

'Yes,' said the lady of the house sadly, 'it is far away. But we will try to help you to get there.' Eliza wanted to go to Canada, because it belonged to the British. They did not allow any one to be made a slave there. George, too, was going to try to reach Canada.

'Wife,' said the gentleman, when they had gone back again into their own sitting-room, 'we must get that poor woman away to-night. She is not safe here. I know some good people, far in the country, who will take care of her.'

So this kind gentleman got the carriage ready, and drove Eliza and her boy a long, long way, through the dark night, to a cottage far in the country. There he left her with a good man and his wife, who promised to be kind to her, and help her to go to Canada. He gave some money to the good man too, and told him to use it for Eliza.

CHAPTER VI

UNCLE TOM SAYS GOOD-BYE

The day after the hunt for Eliza was a very sad one in Uncle Tom's cabin. It was the day on which Haley was going to take Uncle Tom away.

Aunt Chloe had been up very early. She had washed and ironed all Tom's clothes, and packed his trunk neatly. Now she was cooking the breakfast, — the last breakfast she would ever cook for her dear husband. Her eyes were quite red and swollen with crying, and the tears kept running down her cheeks all the time.

'It's the last time,' said Tom sadly.

26

Aunt Chloe could not answer. She sat down, buried her face in her hands, and sobbed aloud.

'S'pose we must be resigned. But, O Lord, how can I? If I knew anything where you was goin', or how they'd treat you! Missis says she'll try and buy you back again in a year or two. But, Lor', nobody never comes back that goes down there.'

'There'll be the same God there, Chloe, that there is here.'

'Well,' said Aunt Chloe, 's'pose dere will. But the Lord lets drefful things happen sometimes. I don't seem to get no comfort dat way.'

'Let's think on our mercies,' said Tom, in a shaking voice.

'Mercies!' said Aunt Chloe, 'don't see any mercies in 't. It isn't right! it isn't right it should be so! Mas'r never ought to have left it so that ye could be took for his debts. Mebbe he can't help himself now, but I feel it's wrong. Nothing can beat that out of me. Such a faithful crittur as ye've been, reckonin' on him more than your own wife and chil'en.'

'Chloe! now, if ye love me, you won't talk so, when it is perhaps jest the last time we'll ever have together,' said Tom.

'Wall, anyway, there's wrong about it somewhere,' said Aunt Chloe, 'I can't jest make out where 'tis. But there is wrong somewhere, I'm sure of that.'

Neither Tom nor Chloe could eat any breakfast; their hearts were too full of sorrow. But the little children, who hardly understood what was happening, enjoyed theirs. It was not often that they had such a fine one as Chloe had cooked for Tom's last morning at home.

Breakfast was just finished, when Mrs. Shelby came. Chloe was not very pleased to see her. She was angry, and blamed her for letting Tom be sold.

But Mrs. Shelby did not seem to see Aunt Chloe's angry looks. 'Tom,' she said, turning to him, 'I come to—' she could say no more, she was crying so bitterly.

Then all Aunt Chloe's anger faded away.

'Lor', now missis, don't-don't,' she said. She too burst out crying again, and for a few minutes they all sobbed together.

'Tom,' said Mrs. Shelby at last, 'I can't do anything for you now. But I promise you, most solemnly, to save as much, money as I can. As soon as I have enough, I will buy you back again.'

Just then Haley arrived. Tom said a last sad good-bye to his wife and children, and got into the cart, which Haley had brought with him.

As soon as Tom was seated in the cart, Haley took a heavy chain, and fastened it round his ankles. Poor Tom had done nothing wrong, yet he was treated worse than a thief, just because he was a slave.

'You don't need to do that,' said Mrs. Shelby, 'Tom won't run away.'

'Don't know so much about that, ma'am; I've lost one already. I can't afford to run any more risks,' replied Haley.

'Please give my love to Mas'r George,' said Tom, looking round sadly. 'Tell him how sorry I am he is not at home to say good-bye.'

Master George was Mr. and Mrs. Shelby's son. He was very fond of Tom, and was teaching him to write. He often used to come and have tea in Uncle Tom's little cottage. Aunt Chloe used to make her very nicest cakes when Mas'r George came to tea. But he was not at home now, and did not know that Tom had been sold.

Haley whipped up the horse, and, with a last sad look at the old place, Tom was whirled away to a town called Washington.

CHAPTER VII

UNCLE TOM MEETS EVA

Haley stayed in Washington several days. He went to market each day and bought more slaves. He put heavy chains on their hands and feet, and sent them to prison along with Tom.

When he had bought all the slaves he wanted, and was ready to go, he drove them before him, like a herd of cattle, on to a boat which was going south.

It was a beautiful boat. The deck was gay with lovely ladies and fine gentlemen walking about enjoying the bright spring sunshine.

Down on the lower deck, in the dark, among the luggage, were crowded Tom and the other poor slaves.

Some of the ladies and gentlemen on board were very sorry for the poor niggers, and pitied them. Others never thought about them at all, or if they did, thought it was quite just and proper that they should be treated badly. 'They are only slaves,' they said.

Among the passengers was a pretty little girl, about six years old. She had beautiful golden hair, and big blue eyes. She ran about here, there, and everywhere, dancing and laughing like a little fairy. There were other children on board, but not one so pretty or so merry as she. She was always dressed in white, and Tom thought she looked like a little angel, as she danced and ran about.

Often and often she would come and walk sadly around the place where the poor slaves sat in their chains. She would look pityingly at them, and then go slowly away. Once or twice she came with her dress full of sweets, nuts, and oranges, and gave them all some.

Tom watched the little lady, and tried to make friends with her. His pockets were full of all kinds of things, with which he used to amuse his old master's children.

He could make whistles of every sort and size, cut baskets out of cherry-stones, faces out of nut-shells, jumping figures out of bits of wood. He brought these out one by one, and though the little girl was shy at first, they soon grew to be great friends.

30

'What is missy's name?' said Tom one day.

'Evangeline St. Clare,' said the little girl; 'though papa and everybody else call me Eva. Now, what's your name?'

'My name's Tom. The little chil'en at my old home used to call me Uncle Tom.'

'Then I mean to call you Uncle Tom, because, you see, I like you,' said Eva. 'So, Uncle Tom, where are you going?'

'I don't know, Miss Eva.'

'Don't know?' said Eva.

'No. I'm going to be sold to somebody. I don't know who.'

'My papa can buy you, said Eva quickly. 'If he buys you you will have good times. I mean to ask him to, this very day.'

'Thank you, my little lady,' said Tom.

Just at this moment, the boat stopped at a small landing-place to take in some wood. Eva heard her father's voice, and ran away to speak to him.

Tom too rose and walked to the side. He was allowed to go about now without chains. He was so good and gentle, that even a man like Haley could not help seeing that it could do no harm to let him go free.

Tom helped the sailors to carry the wood on the boat. He was so big and strong that they were very glad to have his help.

Eva and her father were standing by the railings as the boat once more began to move. It had hardly left the landing-stage when, some how or other, Eva lost her balance. She fell right over the side of the boat into the water.

Tom was standing just under her, on the lower deck, as she fell. In one moment he sprang after her. The next he had caught her his arms, and was swimming with her to the boat-side, where eager hands were held out to take her.

The whole boat was in confusion. Every one ran to help Eva, while the poor slave went back to his place, unnoticed and uncared for.

But Mr. St. Clare did not forget.

The next day Tom sat on the lower deck, with folded arms, anxiously watching him as he talked to Haley.

Eva's father was a very handsome man. He was like Eva, with the same beautiful blue eyes and golden-brown hair. He was very fond of fun and laughter, and though he had quite made up his mind to buy Tom, he was now teasing Haley, and pretending to think that he was asking too much money for him.

'Papa do buy him, it's no matter what you pay', whispered Eva softly, putting her arms around her father's neck. 'You have money enough, I know. I want him.'

'What for, pussy? Are you going to use him for a rattle-box, or a rocking-horse, or what?'

'I want to make him happy.'

Mr. St. Clare laughed; but after making a few more jokes about it, he gave Haley the money he asked for, and Tom had a new master.

'Come, Eva,' said Mr. St. Clare, and, taking her hand, went across the boat to Tom.

'Look up, Tom,' he said to him, 'and see how you like your new master.'

Tom looked up. Mr. St. Clare had such a gay, young, handsome face, that Tom could not help feeling glad. Grateful tears rushed to his eyes as he said, 'God bless you, mas'r.'

'Can you drive horses, Tom?'

'I've been allays used to horses,' said Tom.

'Well, I think I'll make you a coachman. But you must not get drunk.'

Tom looked surprised and a little hurt.

'I never drink', mas'r,' he said.

'Never mind, my boy,' said Mr. St. Clare, seeing him look so grave; 'I don't doubt you mean to do well.'

'I certainly do, mas'r,' said Tom.

'And you shall have good times,' said Eva. 'Papa is very good to everybody, only he always will laugh at them.'

'Papa is much obliged to you,' said Mr. St. Clare laughing, as he walked away.

CHAPTER VIII

ELIZA AMONG THE QUAKERS

While Uncle Tom was sailing South, down the wide river, to his new master's home, Eliza with her boy was travelling north to Canada.

Kind people helped her all the way. She passed from friend to friend, till she arrived safely at a village where the people were Quakers.

The Quakers were gentle, quiet people. They all dressed alike in plain grey clothes, and the women wore big, white muslin caps. Because they thought it was wicked to have slaves, they helped those who ran away from their cruel masters. Often they were punished for doing this, but still they went on helping the poor slaves. For though the laws said it was wrong, they felt quite sure that it was really right to do so.

The kind Quaker women grew to be very fond of Eliza, and would have been glad if she would have stayed with them.

But Eliza said, 'No, I must go on; I dare not stop. I can't sleep at night: I can't rest. Last night I dreamed I saw that man come into the yard.'

'Poor child,' said Rachel, the kind Quaker woman to whom she was speaking, 'poor child, thee mustn't feel so. No slave that has run away has ever been stolen from our village. It is safe here.'

While they were talking, Simeon, Rachel's husband, came to the door and called, 'Wife, I want to speak to thee a minute.'

Rachel went out to him. 'Eliza's husband is here,' he said.

'Art thee sure?' asked Rachel, her face bright with joy.

'Yes, quite certain; he will be here soon. Will thee tell her?'

Rachel went back into the kitchen, where Eliza was sewing, and, opening the door of a small bedroom, said gently, 'Come in here with me, my daughter; I have news to tell thee.'

Eliza rose trembling, she was so afraid it was bad news.

'No, no! never fear thee. It's good news, Eliza,' said Simeon,

Rachel shut the door, and drew Eliza towards her. 'The Lord has been very good to thee,' she said gently. 'Thy husband hath escaped, and will be here to-night.'

'To-night!' repeated Eliza, 'to-night!'

Then it seemed as if the room and everything in it swam round her, and she fell into Rachel's arms.

Very gently Rachel laid her down on the bed. Eliza slept as she had not slept since the dreadful night when she had taken her boy and run away through the cold, dark night.

She dreamed of a beautiful country — a land, it seemed to her, of rest — green shores, pleasant islands, and lovely glittering water. There in a house, which kind voices told her was her home, she saw Harry playing happily. She heard her husband's footstep. She felt him coming nearer. His arms were around her, his tears falling upon her face, and she awoke.

It was no dream. The sun had set, the candles were lit. Harry was sleeping by her side, and George, her husband, was holding her in his arms.

CHAPTER IX

UNCLE TOM'S NEW HOME

Uncle Tom soon settled down in his new home. He was as happy as he could be, so far away from his wife and dear little children. He had a kind master.

Mrs. St. Clare, however, was not nearly so nice as her husband. She was cruel, and would often have beaten her poor slaves, but Mr. St. Clare would not allow it.

She always pretended that she was very ill, and spent most of her time lying on a sofa, or driving about in her comfortable carriage.

Mrs. St. Clare said she really was too ill to look after the house, so everything was left to the slaves. Soon things began to be very uncomfortable, and even good-natured Mr. St. Clare could stand it no longer.

He went to his cousin, Miss Ophelia St. Clare, and begged her to come and keep house for him, and to look after Eva. It was on the journey back with her that the accident to Eva happened, which ended in his buying Tom.

Miss Ophelia was a very prim and precise person, not at all like the St. Clares. In her home people did not have slaves. Though her cousin had a great many, and was kind to them, she could not help seeing that it was a very wicked thing to buy and sell men and women as if they were cattle. She was very, very sorry for the poor slaves, and would have liked to free them all. Yet she did not love them. She could not bear even to have them near her, nor to touch them, just because they were black.

It made her quite ill to see Eva kissing and hugging the black slave women when she came home.

'Well, I couldn't do that,' she said.

'Why not?' said Mr. St. Clare, who was looking on.

'Well, I want to be kind to every one. I wouldn't have anybody hurt. But, as to kissing niggers—' she gave a little shudder. 'How can she?'

Presently a gay laugh sounded from the court. Mr. St. Clare stepped out to see what was happening.

'What is it?' said Miss Ophelia, following him.

There sat Tom on a little mossy seat in the court. Every one of his buttonholes was stuck full of flowers. Eva, laughing gaily, was hanging a wreath of roses round his neck. Then, still laughing, she perched on his knee like a little sparrow.

'Oh, Tom, you look so funny!'

Tom had a sober smile on his face. He seemed in his own quiet way to be enjoying the fun quite as much as his little mistress. When he lifted his eyes and saw his master he looked as if he were afraid he might be scolded. But Mr. St. Clare only smiled.

'How can you let her do that?' said Miss Ophelia.

'Why not?' said Mr. St. Clare.

'Why? I don't know. It seems dreadful to me.'

'You would think it was quite right and natural if you saw Eva playing with a large dog, even if he was black. But a fellow-creature that can think, and reason, and feel, and is immortal, you shudder at. I know how you north-country people feel about it. You loathe the blacks as you would a toad or a snake. Yet you pity them, and are angry because they are often ill-treated.'

'Well, cousin,' said Miss Ophelia thoughtfully, 'I daresay you are right. I suppose I must try to get over my feeling.'

CHAPTER X

UNCLE TOM'S LETTER

Uncle Tom felt that he was indeed very fortunate to have found such a kind master and so good a home. He had nice clothes, plenty of food, and a comfortable room to sleep in. He had no hard, disagreeable work to do. His chief duties were to drive Mrs. St. Clare's carriage when she wanted to go out, and to attend on Eva when she wanted him. He soon grew to love his little mistress very, very much indeed.

Mr. St. Clare too began to find Tom very useful. He was dreadfully careless about money, and his chief servant was just as careless as his master. So between them a great deal was not only spent but wasted.

Mr. Shelby had trusted Tom in everything, and Tom had always been careful of his master's money — as careful as if it had been his own. Waste seemed dreadful to him, and he tried to do something to stop it now.

Mr. St. Clare was not long in finding out how clever Tom was, and soon trusted him as thoroughly as Mr. Shelby had done.

But in spite of all his good fortune, Tom used to long very much to go home to see his dear ones again. He had plenty of spare time, and whenever he had nothing to do he would pull his Bible out of his pocket and try to find comfort in reading it.

But as time went on, Uncle Tom longed more and more for his home. At last one day he had a grand idea. He would write a letter.

Before Uncle Tom was sold, George Shelby had been teaching him to write so he thought he could manage a letter.

He begged a sheet of writing-paper from Eva, and going to his room began to make a rough copy on his slate.

It was very difficult. Poor Uncle Tom found that he had quite forgotten how to make some of the letters. Of those he did remember, he was not quite sure which he ought to use. Yes, it was a very difficult thing indeed.

While he was working away, breathing very hard over it, Eva came behind him, and peeped over his shoulder.

'Oh, Uncle Tom! what funny things you are making there!'

Eva put her little golden head close to Uncle Tom's black one, and the two began a grave and anxious talk over the letter. They were both very earnest, and both very ignorant. But after a great deal of consulting over every word, the writing began, they really thought, to look quite like a proper letter.

'Yes, Uncle Tom, it begins to look beautiful,' said Eva, gazing on it with delight. 'How pleased your wife will be, and the poor little children! Oh, it is a shame that you ever had to go away from them! I mean to ask papa to let you go back, some day.'

'Missis said that she would send down money for me, as soon as they could get it together,' said Tom. 'Young Mas'r George, he said he'd come for me. He gave me this dollar as a sign,' and Tom drew the precious dollar from under his coat.

'Oh, he is sure to come, then,' said Eva, 'I am so glad.'

'I wanted to send a letter, you see, to let 'em know where I was, and tell poor Chloe that I was well off, 'cause she felt so dreadful, poor soul.'

'I say, Tom,' said Mr. St. Clare, coming in at the door at this minute.

Tom and Eva both started.

'What's this?' Mr. St. Clare went on, coming up and looking at the slate.

'Oh, it's Tom's letter. I'm helping him to write it,' said Eva. 'Isn't it nice?'

'I wouldn't discourage either of you,' said her father; 'but I rather think, Tom, you had better let me write your letter for you. I'll do it when I come home from my ride.'

'It is very important that he should write,' said Eva, 'because his mistress is going to send money to buy him back again, you know, papa. He told me they had said so.'

Mr. St. Clare thought in his heart that very likely this meant nothing. He thought it was only one of these things which good-natured people said to their slaves to comfort them when they were taken away from their dear ones to be sold. He did not really believe Mrs. Shelby meant to buy Tom back again. However, he did not say so out loud, but just told Tom to get the horses ready for a ride.

That evening the letter was written, and Uncle Tom carried it joyfully to the post-office.

42

CHAPTER XII

GEORGE FIGHTS FOR FREEDOM

The day after George and Eliza met each other once more at the end of so many sad months of parting, was a very happy one in the Quaker house.

The two had much to say to each other. George had to tell how he had escaped from his cruel master, and how he had followed Eliza all the way and at last found her. Then there were plans to make for going on towards Canada. It was arranged that they should start that night at ten o'clock. 'The pursuers are hard after thee, we must not delay,' said Simeon.

Rachel was happy and busy, packing up food and clothes for them to take on the journey.

Late in the afternoon another Quaker, called Phineas, came with the dreadful news that the wicked men, whom Haley had sent to catch Eliza, were only a few miles away.

So George and Eliza decided to start as soon as it was dark. A little while after supper a large covered waggon drew up before the door. They got in and the waggon drove off.

On and on, all through the dark night they drove. About three o'clock, George heard the click of a horse's hoof coming behind them.

'That's Simeon,' said Phineas, who was driving, as he pulled up the horses to listen.

'Halloa, there, Simeon,' he shouted, 'what news? Are they coming?'

'Yes, right on behind, eight or ten of them.'

'Oh! what shall we do?' groaned Eliza.

But Phineas knew the road well. He lashed the horses till they flew along, the waggon rattling and jumping over the hard road behind them.

On they went till they came to a place where the rocks rose straight up from the road like a wall. It seemed impossible for any one to climb up there. But Phineas knew a way.

He stopped the horses. 'Here, Simeon,' he said, 'take the waggon, and drive on as fast as thou canst, and bring back help. Now follow me,' he said to the others, 'quick, for your lives. Run now, if you you ever did run.'

Quicker than we can say it, they were following him up a tiny narrow path to the top of the rocks, and Simeon was galloping the horses with the empty waggon along the road.

'We are pretty safe here,' said Phineas, when they had reached the top. 'Only one person can come up that path at a time. If any one tries it, shoot him.'

The men who were chasing them had now arrived at the foot of of the rocks. They were led by a big man called Tom Loker, and another mean-looking little man, whom Haley had sent.

After some hunting about, they found the path, and, headed by Tom Loker, began to climb up.

'Come up if you like,' George called out, 'but if you do we will shoot you.'

For answer, the little man took aim at George, and fired.

Eliza screamed, but the shot did not hurt him. It passed close to his hair, nearly touched her cheek, and, struck a tree behind.

Tom Loker came on. George waited until he was near enough, then he fired. The shot hit him in the side. But, though wounded, he would not go back. With a yell like that of a mad bull he came leaping on, and sprang right in among them.

Quakers are not allowed to use guns and pistols, so Phineas had been standing back while George shot. Now he sprang forward. As Tom Loker landed in the middle of them, he gave him a great push, saying, 'Friend, thee isn't wanted here.'

Down fell Tom Loker, down, down the steep side of the rock. He crashed and crackled among trees, bushes, logs, loose stones, till he lay bruised and groaning far below. The fall might have killed him, had it not been broken by his clothes catching on the branches of a large tree.

Cruel people are, very often, cowardly too. When the men saw their leader first wounded, and then thrown down, they all ran away.

Mounting their horses, they rode off as fast as they could, leaving Tom Loker lying on the ground wounded and groaning with pain.

As soon as Phineas and the others saw that the wicked men had really ridden away, they climbed down, meaning to walk along the road till they met Simeon.

They had just reached the bottom, when they saw him coming back with the waggon and two other men.

'Now we are safe,' cried Phineas joyfully.

'Well, do stop then,' said Eliza, 'and do something for that poor man. He is groaning dreadfully.'

'It would be no more than Christian,' said George. 'Let us take him with us.'

They lifted the wounded man gently, as if he had been a friend instead of a cruel enemy, and laid him in the waggon. Then they all set out once more.

A drive of about an hour brought them to a neat farm-house. There the tired travellers were kindly received and given a good breakfast.

Tom Loker was put into a comfortable bed, far cleaner and softer than any he had ever slept in before. George and Eliza walked about the garden hand-in-hand, feeling happy together, and almost safe. They were so near Canada now.

CHAPTER XIII

AUNT DINAH

Miss Ophelia found that it was no easy matter to bring anything like order into the St. Clare household. The slaves had been left to themselves so long, and had grown so untidy, that they were not at all pleased with Miss Feely, as they called her, for trying to make them be tidy. However, she had quite made up her mind that order there must be. She got up at four o'clock in the morning, much to the surprise of the housemaids. All day long she was busy dusting and tidying, till Mrs. St. Clare said it made her tired to see cousin Ophelia so busy.

CHAPTER XIV

TOPSY

One morning, while Miss Ophelia was busy, as usual, she heard Mr. St. Clare calling her from the foot of the stairs.

'Come down here, cousin. I have something to show you.'

'What is it?' said Miss Ophelia, coming down with her sewing in her hand.

'I have bought something for you. See here,' he said, pulling forward a little negro girl of about eight or nine years old.

She was quite black. Her round, shining eyes glittered like glass beads. Her wooly hair was plaited into little tails which stuck out in all directions. Her clothes were dirty and ragged. Miss Ophelia thought she had never seen such a dreadful little girl in all her life.

'Cousin, what in the world have you brought that thing here for?' she asked, in dismay.

'For you to teach, to be sure, and train in the way she should go,' said Mr. St. Clare, laughing. 'Topsy,' he went on, 'this is your new mistress. See, now, that you behave yourself.'

'Yes, mas'r,' said Topsy gravely, but her eyes had a wicked twinkle in them.

'You're going to be good, Topsy, you understand?' said Mr. St. Clare.

'Oh yes, mas'r' said Topsy again, meekly folding her hands, but with another twinkle in her eyes.

'Now cousin, what is this for? Your house is full of these little plagues as it is. I get up in the morning and find one asleep behind the door; see one black head poking out from under the table; another lying on the mat. They tumble over the kitchen floor, so that a body can't put their foot down without treading on them. What on earth did you want to bring this one for?'

'For you to teach, didn't I tell you?'

'I don't want her, I'm sure. I have more to do with them now than I want.'

'Well the fact is, cousin,' said Mr. St. Clare, drawing her aside, 'she belonged to some people who were dreadfully cruel and beat her. I couldn't bear to hear her screaming every day, so I bought her. I will give her to you. Do try and make something of her.'

'Well, I'll do what I can,' said Miss Ophelia. 'She is fearfully dirty, and half naked.'

'Well, take her downstairs, and tell somebody to clean her up, and give her some decent clothes.'

Getting Topsy clean was a very long business. But at last it was done.

Then, sitting down before her, Miss Ophelia began to question her.

'How old are you, Topsy?'

'Dunno, missis,' said she, grinning like an ugly little black doll.

'Don't know how old you are! Did nobody ever tell you? Who was your mother?'

'Never had none,' said Topsy, with another grin.

'Never had any mother! What do you mean? Where were you born?'

'Never was born.'

'You mustn't answer me like that, child,' said Miss Ophelia sternly. 'I am not playing with you. Tell me where you were born, and who your father and mother were.'

'Never was born,' said Topsy again very decidedly. 'Never had no father, nor mother, nor nothin'!'

Miss Ophelia hardly knew what to make of her. 'How long have you lived with your master and mistress, then?' she asked.

'Dunno, missis.'

'Is it a year, or more, or less?'

'Dunno, missis.'

'Have you ever heard anything about God, Topsy?' asked Miss Ophelia next.

Topsy looked puzzled, but kept on grinning.

'Do you know who made you?'

'Nobody as I knows on,' replied Topsy, with a laugh. 'Spect I grow'd. Don't think nobody ever made me.'

'Do you know how to sew?' asked Miss Ophelia, quite shocked.

'No, missis.'

'What can you do? What did you do for your master and mistress?'

'Fetch water, and wash dishes, and clean knives, and wait on folks.'

'Well, now, Topsy, I'm going to show you just how my bed is to be made. I am very particular about my bed. You must learn exactly how to do it.'

'Yes, missis,' said Topsy, with a deep sigh and a face of woeful earnestness.

'Now, Topsy, look here. This is the hem of the sheet. This is the right side of the sheet. This is the wrong. Will you remember?'

'Yes, missis,' said Topsy with another sigh.

'Well, now, the under-sheet you must bring over the bolster — so, and tuck it right down under the mattress nice and smooth—so. Do you see?'

'Yes, missis.'

'But the upper sheet,' said Miss Ophelia, 'must be brought down in this way, and tucked under, firm and smooth, at the foot—so, the narrow hem at the foot.'

'Yes, missis,' said Topsy as before. But while Miss Ophelia was bending over the bed she had quickly seized a pair of gloves and a ribbon, which were lying on the dressing-table, and slipped them up her sleeves. When Miss Ophelia looked up again, the naughty little girl was standing with meekly-folded hand as before.

'Now, Topsy, let me see you do this,' said Miss Ophelia, pulling the clothes off again and seating herself.

Topsy, looking very earnest, did it all just as she had been shown. She did it so quickly and well that Miss Ophelia was very pleased. But, alas! as she was finishing, an end of ribbon came dangling out of her sleeve.

'What is this?' said Miss Ophelia, seizing it. 'You naughty, wicked child—you have been stealing this.'

The ribbon was pulled out of Topsy's own sleeve. Yet she did not seem a bit ashamed. She only looked at it with an air of surprise and innocence.

'Why, that's Miss Feely's ribbon, an't it? How could it a got into my sleeve?'

'Topsy, you naughty girl, don't tell me a lie. You stole that ribbon,'

'Missis, I declare I didn't. Never seed it till dis blessed minnit.'

'Topsy,' said Miss Ophelia, 'don't you know it is wicked to tell lies?'

'I never tells no lies, Miss Feely,' said Topsy. 'It's jist the truth I've been, tellin' now. It an't nothin' else.'

'Topsy, I shall have to whip you, if you tell lies so.'

'Laws, missis, if you whip's all day, couldn't say no other way,' said Topsy, beginning to cry. 'I never seed dat ribbon. It must a caught in my sleeve. Miss Feely must'a left it on the bed, and it got caught in the clothes, and so got in my sleeve.'

Miss Ophelia was so angry at such a barefaced lie that she caught Topsy and shook her. 'Don't tell me that again,' she said.

The shake brought the gloves on the floor from the other sleeve.

'There,' said Miss Ophelia, 'will you tell me now you didn't steal the ribbon?'

Topsy now confessed to stealing the gloves. But she, still said she had not taken the ribbon.

'Now, Topsy', said Miss Ophelia kindly, 'if you will confess all about it I won't whip you this time.'

So Topsy confessed to having stolen both the ribbon and the gloves. She said she was very, very sorry, and would never do it again.

'Well, now, tell me,' said Miss Ophelia, 'have you taken anything else since you have been in the house? If you confess I won't whip you.'

'Laws, missis, I took Miss Eva's red thing she wears on her neck.'

'You did, you naughty child! Well, what else?'

'I took Rosa's ear-rings — them red ones.'

'Go and bring them to me this minute — both of them.'

'Laws, missis, I can't — they's burnt up.'

'Burnt up? What a story! Go and get them, or I shall whip you.'

Topsy began to cry and groan, and declare that she could not. 'They's burnt up, they is.'

'What did you burn them up for?' asked Miss Ophelia.

'Cause I's wicked, I is. I's mighty wicked, anyhow. I can't help it.'

Just at this minute Eva came into the room wearing her coral necklace.

'Why, Eva, where did you get your necklace?' said Miss Ophelia.

'Get it? Why, I have had it on all day,' answered Eva, rather surprised. 'And what is funny, aunty, I had it on all night too. I forgot to take it off when I went to bed.'

Miss Ophelia looked perfectly astonished. She was more astonished still when, next minute, Rosa, who was one of the housemaids, came in with a basket of clean clothes, wearing her coral ear-rings as usual.

I'm sure I don't know what to do with such a child,' she said, in despair. 'What in the world made you tell me you took those things, Topsy?'

'Why, missis said I must 'fess. I couldn't think of nothing else to 'fess,' said Topsy, wiping her eyes.

'But of course, I didn't want you to confess things you didn't do,' said Miss Ophelia. 'That is telling a lie just as much as the other.'

'Laws, now, is it?' said Topsy, looking surprised and innocent.

'Poor Topsy,' said Eva, 'why need you steal? You are going to be taken good care of now. I am sure I would rather give you anything of mine than have you steal

55

it.'

Topsy had never been spoken to so kindly and gently in all her life. For a minute she looked as if she were going to cry. The next she was grinning as usual in her ugly way.

What was to be done with Topsy? Miss Ophelia was quite puzzled. She shut her up in a dark room till she could think about it.

'I don't see,' she said to Mr. St. Clare, 'how I am going to manage that child without whipping her.'

'Well, whip her, then.'

'I never heard of bringing up children without it,' said Miss Ophelia.

'Oh, well, do as you think best. Only, I have seen this child beaten with a poker, knocked down with the shovel or tongs, or anything that came handy. So I don't think your beatings will have much effect.'

'What is to be done with her, then?' said Miss Ophelia. 'I never saw such a child as this.'

But Mr. St. Clare could not answer her question. So Miss Ophelia had to go on, as best she could, trying to make Topsy a good girl.

She taught her to read and to sew. Topsy liked reading, and learned her letters like magic. But she could not bear sewing. So she broke her needles or threw them away. She tangled, broke, and dirtied her cotton and hid her reels. Miss Ophelia felt sure all these things could not be accidents. Yet she could never catch Topsy doing them.

In a very few days Topsy had learned how to do Miss Ophelia's room perfectly, for she was very quick and clever. But if Miss Ophelia ever left her to do it by herself there was sure to be dreadful confusion.

Instead of making the bed, she would amuse herself with pulling off the pillow-cases. Then she would butt her woolly head among the pillows, until it was covered with feathers sticking out in all directions. She would climb the bedpost, and hang head downwards from the top; wave the sheets and covers all over the room; dress the bolster up in Miss Ophelia's nightgown and act scenes with it, singing, whistling, and making faces at herself in the looking-glass all the time.

'Topsy,' Miss Ophelia would say, when her patience was at an end, 'what makes you behave so badly?'

'Dunno, missis—I'spects' cause I's so wicked.'

'I don't know what I shall do with you, Topsy.'

'Laws, missis, you must whip me. My old missis always did. I an't used to workin' unless I gets whipped.'

So Miss Ophelia tried it. Topsy would scream and groan and implore. But half an hour later she would be sitting among the other little niggers belonging to the house, laughing about it. 'Miss Feely whip!' she would say, 'she can't do it nohow.'

'Law, you niggers,' she would go on, 'does you know you's all sinners? Well, you is; everybody is. White folks is sinners too—Miss Feely says so. But I 'spects niggers is the biggest ones. But ye an't any of ye up to me. I's so awful wicked, there can't nobody do nothin' with me. I 'spects I's the wickedest crittur in the world.' Then she would turn a somersault, and come up bright and smiling, evidently quite pleased with herself.

CHAPTER XV

EVA AND TOPSY

Two or three years passed. Uncle Tom was still with Mr. St. Clare, far away from his home. He was not really unhappy. But always in his heart was the aching longing to see his dear ones again.

Now he began to have a new sorrow. He loved his little mistress Eva very tenderly, and she was ill.

He saw that she was growing white and thin. She no longer ran and played in the garden for hours together as she used to do. She was always tired now.

Miss Ophelia noticed it too, and tried to make Mr. St. Clare see it. But he would not. He loved his little Eva so much, that he did not want to believe that anything could be the matter with her.

Mrs. St. Clare never thought that any one, except herself, could be ill. So Eva grew daily thinner and weaker, and Uncle Tom and Aunt Ophelia more and more sad and anxious.

But at last she became so unwell, that even Mr. St. Clare had to own that something was wrong, and the doctor was sent for.

In a week or two she was very much better. Once more she ran about playing and laughing, and her father was delighted. Only Miss Ophelia and the doctor sighed and shook their heads. And little Eva herself knew; but she was not troubled. She knew she was going to God.

'Papa' she said one day, 'there are some things I want to say to you. I want to say them now while I am able.'

She seated herself on his knee, and laid her head on his shoulder.

'It is all no use, papa, to keep it to myself any longer. The time is coming when I am going to leave you. I am going, never to come back', and Eva sobbed.

'Eva, darling, don't say such things; you are better you know.'

'No, papa, I am not any better. I know it quite well, and I am going soon.'

'And I want to go,' she went on, 'only I don't want to leave you – it almost breaks my heart.'

'Don't, Eva, don't talk so. What makes you so sad?'

'I feel sad for our poor people. I wish, papa, they were all free. Isn't there any way to have all slaves made free?'

'That is a difficult question, dearest. There is no doubt that this way is a very bad one. A great many people think so. I do myself. I wish there was not a slave in the land. But then, I don't know what is to be done about it.'

'Papa, you are such a good man, and so noble and kind. Couldn't you go all around and try and persuade people to do right about this? When I am dead, papa, then you will think of me, and do it for my sake.'

'When you are dead, Eva! Oh, child, don't talk to me so.'

'Promise me at least, father, that Tom shall have his freedom, as soon as I am gone.'

'Yes, dear, I will do anything you wish. Only don't talk so.'

Miss Ophelia and Eva had been to church together. Miss Ophelia had gone to her room to take off her bonnet, while Eva talked to her father.

Suddenly Mr. St. Clare and his little girl heard a great noise coming from Miss Ophelia's room. A minute later she appeared, dragging Topsy behind her.

'Come out here' she was saying. 'I will tell your master.'

'What is the matter now?' asked Mr. St. Clare.

'The matter is that I cannot be plagued with this child any longer' said Miss Ophelia. 'It is past all bearing. Here, I locked her up, and gave her a hymn to learn. What does she do, but spy out where I put my key. She has gone to my wardrobe, taken a bonnet-trimming, and cut it all to pieces to make dolls' jackets! I never saw anything like it in my life.'

'I don't know what to do' she went on; 'I have taught and taught. I have talked till I'm tired. I've whipped her. I've punished her in every way I can think of, and still she is as naughty as she was at first.'

'Come here, Topsy, you monkey,' said Mr. St. Clare.

Topsy came, her hard, round eyes glittering and blinking, half in fear, half in mischief.

'What makes you behave so?' said Mr. St. Clare, who could not help being amused at her funny expression.

'Spects it's my wicked heart; Miss Feely says so.'

'Don't you see how much Miss Ophelia has done for you? She says she has done everything she can think of.'

'Lor', yes, mas'r! Old missis used to say so, too. She whipped me a heap harder, and used to pull my hair and knock my head agin the door. But it didn't do me no good. I 'spect if they is to pull every hair out o' my head it wouldn't do no good neither. I's so wicked. Laws! I's nothin' but a nigger noways.'

61

'I shall have to give her up,' said Miss Ophelia. 'I can't have that trouble any longer.'

Eva had stood silent, listening. Now she took Topsy by the hand, and led her into a little room close by.

'What makes you so naughty, Topsy?' she said, with tears in her eyes. 'Why don't you try to be good? Don't you love anybody, Topsy?'

'Dunno nothin' 'bout love. I love candy, that's all.'

'But you love your father and mother?'

'Never had none, ye know. I telled ye that, Miss Eva.'

'Oh, I forgot,' said Eva sadly. 'But hadn't you any brother, or sister or aunt, or —'

'No, none on 'em. Never had nothin' nor nobody.'

'But, Topsy, if you would only try to be good you might —'

'Couldn't never be nothin' but a nigger, if I was ever so good,' said Topsy. 'If I could be skinned, and come white, I'd try then.'

'But people can love you, if you are black, Topsy. Miss Ophelia would love you if you were good.'

Topsy laughed scornfully.

'Don't you think so?' said Eva.

'No. She can't bear me, 'cause I'm a nigger. She'd as soon have a toad touch her. There can't nobody love niggers, and niggers can't do nothin'. I don't care,' and Topsy began whistling to show that she didn't.

'Oh, Topsy! I love you,' said Eva, laying her little, thin hand on Topsy's shoulder. 'I love you, because you haven't had any mother, or father, or friends; because you have been a poor, ill-used child. I love you, and I want you to be good. It makes me sorry to have you so naughty. I wish you would try to be good for my sake, because I'm going to die soon. I shan't be here very long.'

Topsy's round, bright eyes grew suddenly dim with tears. She did believe at last that it was possible for some one to love her. She laid her head down between her knees and wept and sobbed.

'Poor Topsy,' said Eva gently.

'Oh, Miss Eva, dear Miss Eva,' cried the poor little black child, 'I will try, I will try. I never did care nothin' about it before.'

CHAPTER XVI

EVA'S LAST GOOD-BYE

It soon became quite plain to everybody that Eva was very ill indeed. She never ran about and played now, but spent most of the day lying on the sofa in her own pretty room.

Every one loved her, and tried to do things for her. Even naughty little Topsy used to bring her flowers, and try to be good for her sake.

Uncle Tom was a great deal in Eva's room. She used to get very restless, and then she liked to be carried about. He was so big and strong that he could do it very easily. He would walk about with her under the orange-trees in the garden, or sitting down on some of their old seats, would sing their favorite hymns.

He loved to do it, and could not bear to be long away from his little mistress. He gave up sleeping in his bed, and lay all night on the mat outside her door.

One day Eva made her aunt cut off a lot of her beautiful hair. Then she called all the slaves together, said good-bye to them, and gave them each a curl of her hair as a keepsake. They all cried very much, and said they would never forget her, and would try to be good for her sake.

A few nights later Miss Ophelia came quickly to Tom, as he lay on the mat outside Eva's door. 'Go, Tom,' she said, 'go as fast as you can for the doctor.'

Tom ran. But in the morning little Eva lay on her bed, cold and white, with closed eyes and folded hands.

She had gone to God.

Mr. St. Clare was very, very unhappy for a long time after Eva died. He had loved her so much, that now his life seemed quite empty without her.

He did not forget his promise to her about Tom. He went to his lawyer, and told him to begin writing out the papers that would make Tom free. It took some time to make a slave free.

'Well, Tom,' said Mr. St. Clare the day after he had spoken to his Lawyer, 'I'm going to make a free man of you. So have your trunk packed and get ready to set out for home.'

Joy shone in Uncle Tom's face. 'Bless the Lord,' he said, raising his hands to heaven.

Mr. St. Clare felt rather hurt. He did not like Tom to be so glad to leave him.

'You haven't had such a very bad time here that you need be in such rapture, Tom,' he said.

'No, no, mas'r! tan't that. It's bein' a free man! That's what I'm joyin' for.'

'Why, Tom, don't you think that you are really better off as you are?'

'No, indeed, Mas'r St. Clare,' said Tom, very decidedly; 'no, indeed.'

'But, Tom, you couldn't possibly have earned by your work such clothes and such nice, comfortable rooms and good food as I have given you.'

'I knows all that, Mas'r St. Clare. Mas'r has been too good. But, mas'r, I'd rather have poor clothes, poor house, poor everything, and have 'em mine than have the best, and have 'em any man's else. I had so, mas'r. I thinks it's nature, mas'r.'

'I suppose so, Tom. You will be going off and leaving me, in a month or two,' he said, rather discontentedly. 'Though why you shouldn't, I don't know,' he added, in a gayer voice.

'Not while mas'r is in trouble,' said Tom. 'I'll stay with mas'r as long as he wants me — so as I can be of any use.'

'Not while I am in trouble, Tom?' said Mr. St. Clare, looking sadly out of the window. 'And when will my trouble be over?' Then half-smiling he turned from the window, and laid his hand on Tom's shoulder. 'Ah, Tom, you soft, silly boy,' he said. 'I won't keep you. Go home to your wife and children, and give them all my love.'

'Cousin,' said Miss Ophelia, coming into the room, 'I want to speak to you about Topsy.'

'What has she been doing now?'

'Nothing; she is a much better girl than she used to be. But I want to ask you, whose is she—yours or mine?'

'Why yours, of course; I gave her to you,' said Mr. St. Clare.

'But not by law. There is no use my trying to make this child a Christian, unless I can be quite sure that she will not be sold as a slave again. If you are really willing I should have her, I want you to give me a paper saying she is mine.'

'But you think it is wicked to keep slaves. Now you want to have one of your own. Oh! shocking, cousin,' said Mr. St. Clare, who loved to tease.

'Nonsense! I only want to have her, so that I can set her free.'

'Very well,' said Mr. St. Clare, 'I will write the paper for you.' Then he sat down and began to read.

'But I want it done now,' said Miss Ophelia.

'Why are you in such a hurry?'

'Because now is the only time there ever is to do a thing in,' said Miss Ophelia. 'want to make sure of it. You may die or lose all your money. Then Topsy would be taken away and sold, in spite of anything I could say.'

Mr. St. Clare hated being made to do things when he didn't want to. However, after teasing his cousin a little more, he wrote out the paper, and Topsy belonged to Miss Ophelia. That evening Mr. St. Clare went out for a ride.

Tom saw him go, and asked if he should come too. 'No, my boy,' said Mr. St. Clare, 'I shall be back in an hour.'

Tom sat down on the verandah to wait till his master came home. While he waited, he fell asleep.

Presently he was awakened by loud knocking, and the sound of voices at the gate.

He ran to open it.

Several men were there carrying a load. It was Mr. St. Clare. He had been hurt in an accident, and was dying.

Very gently they laid him on a sofa. Nothing could be done. In a short time he had gone to join his little Eva.

CHAPTER XVII

UNCLE TOM'S NEW MASTER

There had been great grief in the house when Eva died. Now there was not only sorrow, but gloom and fear.

The kind master was dead, and the poor slaves asked themselves in despair what would happen to them now.

They were not long left in doubt. One morning Mrs. St. Clare told them that they were all to be sold. She was going back to her father's house to live, and would not want them any more.

Poor Uncle Tom! The news was a dreadful blow to him. For a few days he had been so happy in the thought of going home. Once more, after all these years, he thought he would see his dear wife and little children. Now, at one stroke, he had lost both his kind master and his hope of freedom.

Instead of going home, he was to be sent farther away than ever from his dear ones. He could not bear it. He tried to say, "Thy will be done", but bitter tears almost choked the words.

He had one hope left. He would ask Miss Ophelia to speak to Mrs. St. Clare for him.

'Mas'r St. Clare promised me my freedom, Miss Feely,' he said. 'He told me that he had begun to take it out for me. And now, perhaps, if you would be good enough to speak about it to missis, she would feel like going on with it. Seeing it was Mas'r St. Clare's wish, she might.'

'I'll speak for you, Tom, and do my best,' said Miss Ophelia. 'I haven't much hope, but I will try.'

So Miss Ophelia asked Mrs. St. Clare to set Tom free.

'Indeed, I shall do no such thing,' she replied. 'Tom is worth more than any of the other slaves. I couldn't afford to lose so much money. Besides, what does he want with his freedom? He is a great deal better off as he is.'

'But he does want it very much,' replied Miss Ophelia. 'And his master promised it to him.'

'I dare say he does want it,' replied Mrs. St. Clare. 'They all want it. Just because they are a discontented set, always wanting what they haven't got.'

'But Tom is so good and gentle, and such a splendid worker. If you sell him there is the chance of his getting a bad master.'

'Oh, I have no fear about that. Most masters are good, in spite of all the talk people make about it,' replied Mrs. St. Clare.

'Well', said Miss Ophelia at last, 'I know it was one of the last wishes of your husband that Tom should have his freedom. He promised dear little Eva that he should have it. I think you ought to do it.'

Then Mrs. St. Clare began to cry, and say every one was unkind to her, and Miss Ophelia saw it was no use saying anything more. There was only one other thing she could do. She wrote to Mrs. Shelby, telling her that poor Uncle Tom was going to be sold again. She asked her to send money to buy him back, as soon as possible.

The next day, Uncle Tom and the other slaves belonging to Mr. St. Clare were

70

sent to market to be sold.

As Uncle Tom stood in the market-place, waiting for some one to buy him, he looked anxiously round. In the crowd of faces, he was trying to find one kind, handsome one, like Mr. St. Clare's. But there was none.

Presently a short, broad man, with a coarse, ugly face and dirty hands, came up to Tom. He looked him all over, pulled his mouth open and looked at his teeth, pinched his arms, made him walk and jump, and indeed treated him as he would a horse or cow he had wished to buy.

Tom knew from the way this man looked and spoke, that he must be bad and cruel. He prayed in his heart that this might not be his new master. But it was. His name was Legree. He bought Uncle Tom, several other men slaves, and two women. One of the women was a pretty young girl, who had never been away from her mother before, and who was very much afraid of her new master. The other was an old woman. The two women were chained together. The men, Uncle Tom among them, had heavy chains put on both hands and feet. Then Legree drove them all on to a boat which was going up the river to his plantation.

It was a sad journey. This time there was no pretty Eva, nor kind-hearted Mr. St. Clare, to bring any happiness to the poor slaves.

One of the first things Legree did was to take away all Tom's nice clothes which Mr. St. Clare had given him.

He made him put on his oldest clothes, then he sold all the others to the sailors.

Legree made his slaves unhappy in every way he could think of. Then he would come up to them and say, 'Come, come, I don't allow any sulky looks. Be

71

cheerful, now, or—' and he would crack his whip in a way to make them
tremble.

At last the weary journey was over. Legree and his slaves landed. His house was
a long way from the river. The men slaves walked, while Legree and the two
women drove in a cart.

Mile after mile they trudged along, over the rough road through wild and dreary
country, till, hungry, thirsty, and tired, they arrived at the farm, or plantation as
it was called.

Legree was not a gentleman like Mr. Shelby or Mr. St. Clare. He was a very
rough kind of farmer. On his farm he grew cotton. The cotton had to be gathered
and tied into bundles. Then he sold it to people who made it into calico, muslin,
and other things, which we need to use and wear. Gathering cotton is very hard
work.

The house Legree lived in had once been a very fine one, and had belonged to a
rich gentleman. Now, it was old, neglected, and almost in ruins.

The house was bad enough, but the cabins where the slaves lived were far worse.
They were roughly built of wood. The wind and the rain came through the
chinks between the planks. There were no windows. The floors were nothing but
the bare earth. There was no furniture of any kind in them, only heaps of dirty
straw to sleep upon.

Uncle Tom felt more unhappy than ever. He had hoped at least to have a little
room which he could keep clean and tidy. But this hole he did not even have to
himself. He had to share it with five or six others.

Now began the saddest time of Uncle Tom's life. Every morning very early the slaves were driven out into the fields like cattle. All day long they worked hard. The burning sun blazed down upon them, making them hot and tired. Legree and his two chief slaves, called Quimbo and Sambo, marched about all the time with whips in their hands. At night they drove the slaves back again to their miserable huts.

But before they could rest, they had to grind and cook the corn for their supper. When at last they did go to sleep, they had to lie on the heaps of dirty straw instead of in comfortable beds.

CHAPTER XVIII

GEORGE AND ELIZA FIND FREEDOM

Tom Loker lay tossing and tumbling in his clean, comfortable bed at the Quaker farmhouse. A pretty, old Quaker lady, with white hair and a kind face, was nursing him. Tom Loker did not like being ill and having to lie in bed. He threw the clothes about, grumbling and using naughty words all the tune.

'I must ask thee, Thomas Loker, not to use such language,' said the nice lady, as she smoothed his sheets, and made his bed comfortable again for him.

'Well, I won't, granny, if I can help it,' he replied; 'but it is enough to make a fellow swear, it is so awfully hot.' He gave another great lunge, and made the sheets and blankets all untidy again.

'I suppose that fellow George and the girl Eliza are here,' he said, in a sulky voice, after a few minutes' silence.

'Yes, they are,' said the old lady.

'They had better get away across the lake,' said Tom Loker, 'the quicker the better.'

'Very likely they will do so,' said the old lady, calmly going on with her knitting.

'But, listen,' said Tom Loker, getting excited, 'there are people who are watching the boats for us. I don't care if I tell now. I hope they will get away, just to spite the others for going and leaving me as they did — the mean puppies, the — '

'Thomas Loker!' said the old lady.

'I tell you, granny, if you bottle a fellow up too tight he'll split,' said Tom Loker. 'But about Eliza — tell them to dress her up some way so as to alter her. We have sent a description of what she looks like to the town where the boats start from. She will be caught yet if she doesn't dress up differently.'

'I thank thee, Thomas Loker,' replied the old lady with her usual calmness. 'We will attend to that. Thank thee.' Then she went to tell George and Eliza what Tom Loker had said.

They were indeed very grateful to him, and very glad that they had not left him, as his own friends had done, to die by the roadside.

So next day Eliza cut off all her beautiful black hair, and dressed herself like a boy.

'Don't I make a pretty young fellow?' she said to George, laughing and blushing at the same time.

'You always will be pretty,' said George gravely, 'do what you will.'

'What makes you so sober?' asked Eliza, kneeling on one knee, and laying her hand on his. 'We are within twenty-four hours of Canada, they say. Only a day and a night on the lake, and then — oh, then!'

'O Eliza,' said George, holding her fast, 'that is just it. To be so near liberty, to be almost in sight of it — and then if we lost it. O Eliza, I should die.'

'Don't fear,' said Eliza hopefully. 'The good Lord would not have brought us so far if He didn't mean to save us. I seem to feel him with us, George.'

So George kissed his wife and took heart again. Then the kind old lady brought Harry in dressed as a little girl. And a very pretty girl he made too. They called him 'Harriet,' as it was so like Harry it was easy to remember.

Harry did not know his mamma, dressed as she was, and clung to the kind lady, feeling rather afraid of the strange young man. That was just as well, as he was too young to understand what this dressing-up and pretending meant, and he might have spoiled it all by calling the nice-looking young man 'Mamma.' So the kind lady was going with them, pretending to be the little girl's aunt.

When everything was ready they got into a cab, and drove to the wharf. The two young men, as they seemed to be, got out, Eliza helping the kind lady and little girl, while George saw to the luggage.

As he was standing at the office, taking the tickets, George overheard two men talking by his side.

'I've watched every one that came on board,' said one, 'and I know they are not on this boat.'

'You would scarcely know the woman from a white one,' said the other. 'The man is very fair too. He has an H burned into the palm of his hand.'

The hand with which George was taking the tickets and change trembled a little, but he turned calmly round, looked straight at the speaker, and then walked slowly away to where Eliza was waiting for him.

It was a terribly anxious time, but at last the bell rang, the boat began to move, and George and Eliza drew long sighs of relief as they saw the shore getting farther and farther away.

It was a lovely day. The blue waves of Lake Erie danced, rippling and sparkling, in the sunlight. Hour after hour the boat steamed on.

Night came; and in the morning, clear and beautiful before them, rose the shores of Canada.

George and his wife stood arm in arm as the boat came near the little town, where they were going to land. His breath came thick and short; a mist gathered before his eyes; he silently pressed the little hand that lay trembling on his arm.

The bell rang—the boat stopped.

Scarcely seeing what he did, George looked out his luggage, and gathered his little party.

They were landed on the shore, and stood still till the boat had started again.

Then with tears of joy, the husband and wife, with their wondering little boy in their arms, knelt down and lifted up their hearts to God. They were free.

CHAPTER XIX

UNCLE TOM FINDS FREEDOM

The letter which Miss Ophelia wrote to Mrs. Shelby, telling her that Tom was to be sold again, was delayed a long time in the post. When at last it did arrive, Mr. Shelby was very ill, and though Mrs. Shelby felt dreadfully sorry about Uncle Tom, she could do nothing, as her husband was so ill. Soon Mr. Shelby died. Mrs. Shelby was very sad, but in her sorrow she did not forget her promise to Aunt Chloe and Uncle Tom. As soon as she could, she sold some land, and George Shelby, taking the money with him, went off to try to find Uncle Tom and buy him back again.

But by the time George Shelby, came to the place where Mr. St. Clare used to live, Uncle Tom had been sold to Legree, and no one knew where he had gone.

At last, after searching about for months, George Shelby found out where Uncle Tom was, and followed him.

Two days after Legree had been so cruel, George Shelby drove up the avenue and stopped at the door of the old house.

'I hear,' he said to Legree, 'that you bought a slave named Tom. He used to belong to my father. I have come to buy him back again.'

Legree's face grew black with anger. 'Yes, I did buy such a fellow,' he growled in rage. 'And a bad bargain it was, too! The most rebellious, saucy, impudent dog! Set up my niggers to run away. He owned to it, and, when I bid him tell me where they were, he said he knew, but wouldn't tell. He stuck to it, too, though I gave him the very worst beating I ever gave a nigger yet. I believe he is trying to die. I shouldn't wonder if he did.'

'Where is he?' said George. 'Let me see him.' His cheeks were crimson, and his eye flashed fire at the thought that Legree had dared to treat dear Uncle Tom so badly.

'He is in that shed,' said a little fellow who was holding George Shelby's horse.

George, without saying another word, hurried to the place to which the little boy pointed.

As he entered the shed, his head felt giddy and his heart sick.

Uncle Tom lay on a heap of straw on the floor, still and quiet.

'Oh, dear Uncle Tom,' cried George as he knelt beside him, 'dear Uncle Tom, do wake—do speak once more. Here's Mas'r George—your own little Mas'r George. Don't you know me?'

'Mas'r George!' said Tom, opening his eyes, and speaking in a feeble voice. 'Mas'r George? it is—it is. It's all I wanted. They haven't forgot me. It warms my soul; it does my old heart good. Now I shall die content.'

'You shan't die! you mustn't die, nor think of it. I've come to buy you and take you home,' said George, and the tears came into his eyes as he bent over poor Uncle Tom.

'Oh, Mas'r George, ye're too late. The Lord has bought me, and is going to take me home.'

'Oh, don't. It breaks my heart to think of what you've suffered—lying in this old shed, too.'

'You mustn't, now, tell Chloe, poor soul, how ye found me,' said Tom, taking George by the hand. 'It would seem so dreadful to her. Only tell her ye found me going into glory, and that I couldn't stay for no one. And oh, the poor chil'en, and the baby—my old heart's been most broke for them. Tell them to follow me. Give my love to mas'r, and dear, good missis, and everybody in the place. I love them all.'

He closed his eyes, and with a smile he fell asleep. Uncle Tom too was free.

Beyond the gates of Legree's farm, George had noticed a dry, sandy knoll, shaded by a few trees. There he made Uncle Tom's grave. No stone marks his last resting-place. He needs none. God knows where he lies.

Kneeling there George bent his head, in shame and sorrow. 'Here me, dear God,' he said, 'from this day, I will do what one man can to drive out the curse of slavery from this land.'

CHAPTER XX

GEORGE SHELBY FREES HIS SLAVES

George Shelby wrote a little note to his mother, telling her that he was coming home. He tried to write about Uncle Tom, but he could not; tears blinded him, and sobs choked him.

On the day he was expected every one was in a state of bustle and excitement. Aunt Chloe in a new print dress, and clean white apron walked round the supper-table, making sure that everything was right. Her black face shone with joy at the thought of seeing Uncle Tom again.

'I'm thinking my old man won't know the boys and the baby,' she said.

Mrs. Shelby sighed. Ever since the letter had come from George she had had a very sad heart. She felt sure something must be wrong.

'He won't know the baby, my old man won't,' said Chloe again, 'Why, it's five years since they took him.'

Just then the sound of wheels was heard.

'It's Mas'r George,' cried Aunt Chloe, running to the window in great excitement.

Mrs. Shelby ran to the door. As George met her he put his arms round her, and kissed her tenderly.

Aunt Chloe stood behind anxiously looking out into the darkness.

'Oh, poor Aunt Chloe,' said George, gently taking her hard, black hand between both his own. 'I'd have given all my fortune to have brought Uncle Tom home with me; but he has gone to a better country.' Mrs. Shelby cried out as if she had been hurt, but Aunt Chloe did not make a sound.

In silence they went into the supper-room.

'There,' said Aunt Chloe, holding out her trembling hands to her mistress, 'it's just as I knew it would be. He's been sold and murdered on dem old plantations.'

Then she turned and walked proudly out of the room. Mrs. Shelby followed her softly, took one of her hands, drew her down into a chair, and sat down beside her.

'My poor, good Chloe,' she said gently.

Chloe leaned her head on her mistress's shoulder, and sobbed out, 'Oh, missis, 'scuse me, my heart's broke—dat's all.'

'I know it is,' said Mrs. Shelby, as her tears fell fast, 'and I cannot heal it.'

There was silence for a little as they wept together. Then George sat down beside Aunt Chloe, and took her hand. He talked gently to her, telling her of Uncle Tom's last loving messages. So she was comforted a little.

One morning, about a month after this, George Shelby called all his servants together, telling them he had something to say to them.

They wondered what it could be, and were very much surprised when he appeared, carrying a bundle of papers in his hand.

They were still more astonished when he gave a paper to each one, and told them all that they were free.

With sobs and tears and shouts they pressed round him, thanking and blessing him. But some of them came with anxious faces, begging him to take their free papers back again, and not to send them away.

'We don't want to be any freer than we are,' they said. 'We have always had all we wanted.'

82

'We don't want to leave the old place, and young mas'r and Missis, and the rest.'

'My good friends,' said George, when he could get silence, 'there will be no need for you to leave me. We want quite as many servants as we did before. But now you are free men and free women. I shall pay you wages for your work, and if I die, or get into debt, you can't be taken away to be sold. That is all the difference. I want you all to stay with me, for I want to teach you how to live as free men and women ought.'

'One thing more,' added George, when the cheering and rejoicing had died away a little. 'You all remember our good old Uncle Tom. You have heard how he died, and how he sent his love to you all. It was on his grave, my friends, that I made up my mind, with God's help, never to own another slave, if it were possible to free him. I resolved that nobody, through my fault, should ever run the risk of being parted from his dear ones, and of dying far from them, as he died.

'So, when you rejoice in your freedom, remember that you owe it to dear old Uncle Tom, and pay it back in kindness to his wife and children. Think of your freedom every time you see Uncle Tom's Cabin; and let it help you to try to live as he did, and be as honest and faithful and Christian as he was.'

THE END.

Made in the USA
Middletown, DE
13 July 2023

35091713R00046